How to Use Nursery Rhymes

Learning with Nursery Rhymes presents twelve popular rhymes and then provides ideas and props for teaching with these rhymes. Follow these basic steps in presenting each rhyme:

Learn the Rhyme
- Read the verse several times.
- Have students echo the verse one line at a time.
- Recite the verse, stopping frequently to have the class fill in the next word or the next line.
- Use illustrations or puppets to help give meaning to the words.

Retell the Rhyme
- Have students become the characters and act out the rhyme.
- Use puppets, picture cards, headbands, and dress-up clothing to retell the story of the rhyme.

Extend the Learning
- Use the rhyme picture cards to reinforce readiness skills.
- Create new stories and rhymes.
- Connect the happenings in the rhyme to happenings in your students' world.

When to Use Nursery Rhymes

Circle Time is a perfect time to introduce a new rhyme, but any time is a good time for a rhyme. You might:

- Recite a rhyme to greet your students.
- Read a book about a rhyme.
- Sing a rhyme at snack time.
- Dismiss your students with familiar lines.

Repeat the rhymes often. Have students tell rhymes that they have learned from their parents and invite parents to visit and teach new rhymes. Create a special class album of favorite rhymes.

How to Use This Book

The Rhyme Page
- Reproduce the page and post the rhyme in the classroom. (You may want to enlarge it to chart size.)
- Make a transparency and use it with an overhead projector. Point to and follow the words as the verse is recited.
- Make a class book by reproducing the rhyme page and adding students' illustrations.

Headbands
- Make the headbands and use them to retell the story of the rhyme.
- Set up a center for dramatic play with the headbands.

Puppets
- Create one set of puppets to help you as you present the rhyme.
- Create a set of puppets for each student and have them act out the story with their puppets.
- Create a new story with the characters in the rhyme.
- Ask and answer questions about the rhyme.

Picture Cards
- Present the rhyme using the cards.
- Retell the rhyme using the cards.
- Sequence the cards to tell the story.

Word Cards
- Add to your "print-rich" environment by using word cards with the retelling of each rhyme.
- Use word cards along with your simple oral directions.
    "Stand up." (show the word card for up)

Manipulatives and Record Sheets
- Use props from the rhymes for counting, sorting, and one-to-one correspondence.
- Observe real animals and compare them to the characters in the rhymes.

Note: A "Know Your Rhymes" record card is included on page 111. Use this in conjunction with rhyme pictures on page 112.
- Use the card to track rhymes learned
- Have each student glue the rhyme pictures in random order on the card. You will have a set of nursery rhyme bingo cards. Enjoy!

Little Robin Redbreast

Little Robin Redbreast sat upon a tree,

Up went the Pussy-Cat, and down went he,

Down came Pussy-Cat, away Robin ran;

Says little Robin Redbreast: "Catch me if you can!"

Little Robin Redbreast sat upon a spade,

Pussy-Cat jumped after him, and then he was afraid.

Little Robin chirped and sang, and what did Pussy say?

Pussy-Cat said: "Mew, mew, mew,"

and Robin flew away.

Little Robin Redbreast was one of the first Mother Goose rhymes published. In the first version, found in *Tommy Thumb's Pretty Song Book* published in 1744, the cat outsmarts the robin. In 1800 Robert Birchall, an English composer, wrote a song using the version of the rhyme written here where the robin is the ultimate winner.

Using Little Robin Redbreast in your Classroom

LANGUAGE ARTS

Retelling the story:
1. Make the two headbands (patterns on pages 6 and 7) representing the robin and the cat.
2. Choose two students to wear the headbands. Ask the students to act out the events in the story as you tell them.
3. Have a student tell the story as other students become the robin and the cat.

Sequencing events:
1. Reproduce the Robin Redbreast picture cards on pages 8-10. You may want to mount them on cardboard or construction paper and laminate them for durability.
2. Tell the rhyme story and show the picture cards in order. Then mix up the cards and have students put them in order.
3. After you have sequenced the pictures as a class, use the cards as a center. Encourage students to recite the rhyme and put the cards in order.

Developing vocabulary:
1. Discuss any words in the rhyme that may be unfamiliar to your students. Relate the words' meanings to your students' lives. For example, you might say, "Have you ever dug a hole in the dirt with a shovel? Another word for shovel is spade."

2. Help students learn to read the words "up" and "down" by reproducing the word cards on page 11.
    • Give simple directions orally, using the word cards at the same time.
        "Stand up." - *up card*
        "Put your book down." - *down card*
    • When your students are ready, use the cards alone to foster their sight word vocabulary.

Little Robin Redbreast illustrated by Shari Halpern (North-South Books, 1994) is a great addition to your classroom library.

MATHEMATICS

Counting:

Reproduce the pictures of the cat and robin on page 12 and the record sheet on page 13.
Look at the cat and count its features.

"How many legs does a cat have?"
"How many ears does a cat have?"

Do the same thing for the robin.
Record the results of your counting on the record sheet.

Cat	How many?	Bird
IIII	Legs	II
I	Tails	I
I	Heads	I
O	Wings	II
II	Ears	II
IIII	Whiskers	O
II	Eyes	II

Count the Cat

Count the Robin

Count and Compare

Comparing:

Spend some time comparing the two animals.
Talk about more and less. If your students are ready use numbers for comparison.

"The cat has more legs than the bird."
"The cat has two more legs than the bird."

SCIENCE

Observation:

Do you have an animal in your classroom? If not, invite a guest fish, hamster, or bird for the day.
Watch quietly and record some of the things it does. Students can draw their observations
on the form on page 14. Or you can make an overhead transparency of the form and write
students' observations in words.

"Look at the hamster stuff all the food in its mouth."
"Now it's running in its wheel."

Use these observations as the basis for discussing the animal's behavior.
Then think about the robin's and the cat's behavior in the rhyme.
Which behaviors could really be observed by watching quietly?
Did the robin or the cat do anything that would not really happen?

(When the robin said, "Catch me if you can.")

Robin Redbreast Headband

1. Cut out the headband.
2. Cut two additional strips 2" x 4" (5 x 10 cm) from construction paper. Paste one to each end of the headband.
3. Insert a paper fastener near each end of the extensions. Loop the ends of a rubber band around the head of each fastener to allow for variations in fit.

Learning with Nursery Rhymes • EMC 741

Pussy-Cat Headband

1. Cut out the headband.
2. Cut two additional strips 2" x 4" (5 x 10 cm) from construction paper. Paste to ends of headband.
3. Insert a paper fastener near each end. Loop the ends of a rubber band around the head of each fastener to allow for variations in fit.

     Learning with Nursery Rhymes • EMC 741

Robin Redbreast Picture Cards

 Learning with Nursery Rhymes • EMC 741

9

down

up

Count the Cat

Count the Robin

Count and Compare

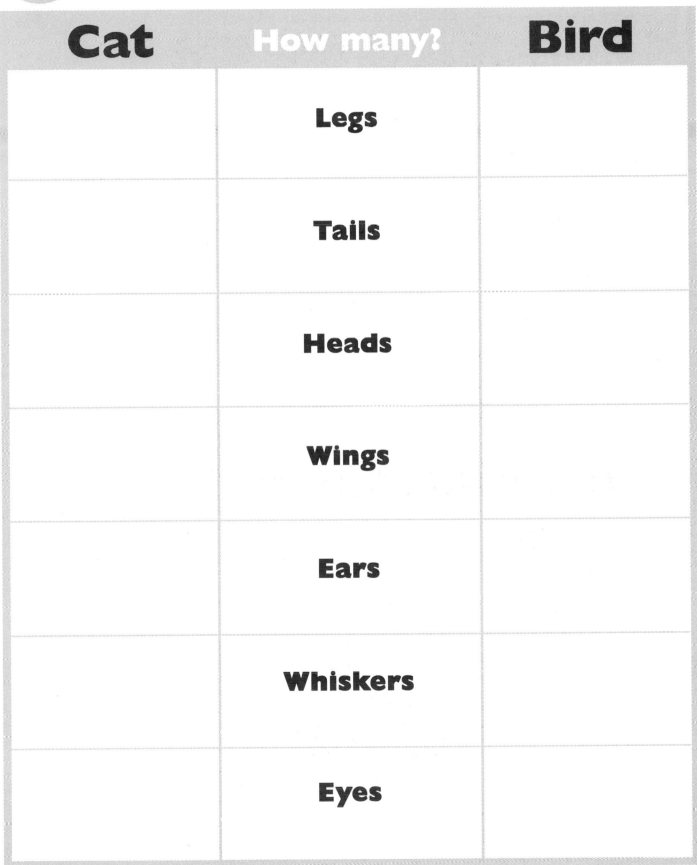

Cat	How many?	Bird
	Legs	
	Tails	
	Heads	
	Wings	
	Ears	
	Whiskers	
	Eyes	

 Learning with Nursery Rhymes • EMC 741

Watching Quietly

What I Saw...

The Noble Duke of York

Oh, the noble Duke of York,

He had ten thousand men.

He marched them up to the top of the hill,

And he marched them down again.

And when they were up, they were up.

And when they were down, they were down.

And when they were only halfway up,

They were neither up nor down.

This British rhyme probably refers to Frederick Augustus, the Duke of York. He was the second son of England's King George III. He fought a battle on a hill in Belgium called Mount Cassel.

Using the Noble Duke of York in your Classroom

LANGUAGE ARTS

Following directions:

After presenting and learning the rhyme, try singing it to the traditional tune. If you don't know the tune, you can find it in *The Lap-Time Song and Play Book* edited by Jane Yolen (Harcourt Brace Jovanovich, 1989).

Then sing and act out the rhyme by standing every time the Duke is marching his men up and sitting when he marches them down.

Developing vocabulary:

Reproduce the Duke of York slider (pages 17-18) for every student.
(The slit in the hill will need to be cut by an adult.)
Have students color, cut, and paste to finish the slider.
Then recite the verse using the slider to show the actions of the soldiers.

Use word cards for up and down (page 11) when students are ready.
Students then move the slider in the direction the word indicates.

MATH

Wholes and parts:

1. Reproduce the puzzle on pages 19-20.
2. Mount the pieces on heavy card stock, cut them apart, and laminate them.
3. Before students put the puzzle together, explain that the completed soldier is a whole. The head, the arm, the leg, and the bodies are parts. When all the parts are put together you have a whole.

Counting:

1. Reproduce the soldier counters on page 21 and the hill on page 22 for each student.
2. Designate different numbers of soldiers and have students place that number either on the top or at the bottom of the hill.

Beginning computation:

Put several soldiers at the top of the hill and several soldiers at the bottom of the hill.
Have students count how many are on the top, on the bottom, and in all.
Write the number sentence with your students if they are ready.

Duke of York

Oh, the noble Duke of York,
He had ten thousand men.
He marched them up to the top of the hill,
And he marched them down again.

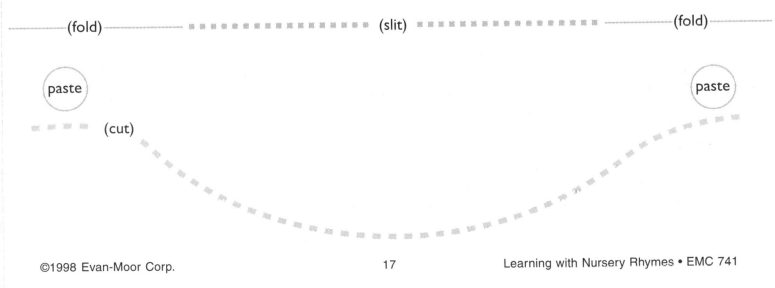

(fold) ---- (slit) ---- (fold)

paste   paste

---- (cut)

Learning with Nursery Rhymes • EMC 741

Duke of York

(cut)

(fold)

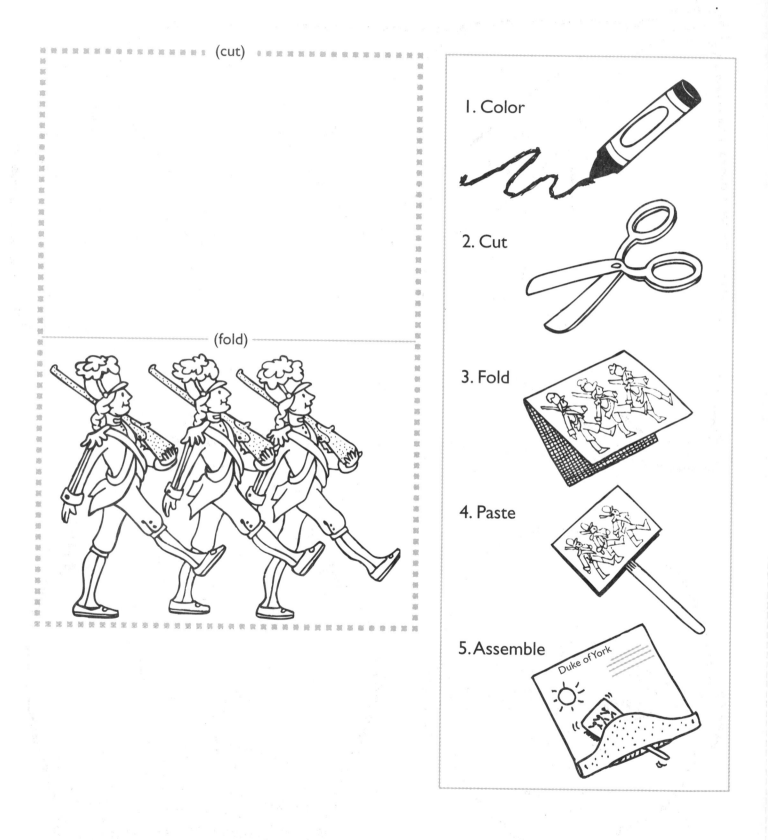

1. Color

2. Cut

3. Fold

4. Paste

5. Assemble

Duke of York

Learning with Nursery Rhymes • EMC 741

Duke of York Puzzle

Learning with Nursery Rhymes • EMC 741

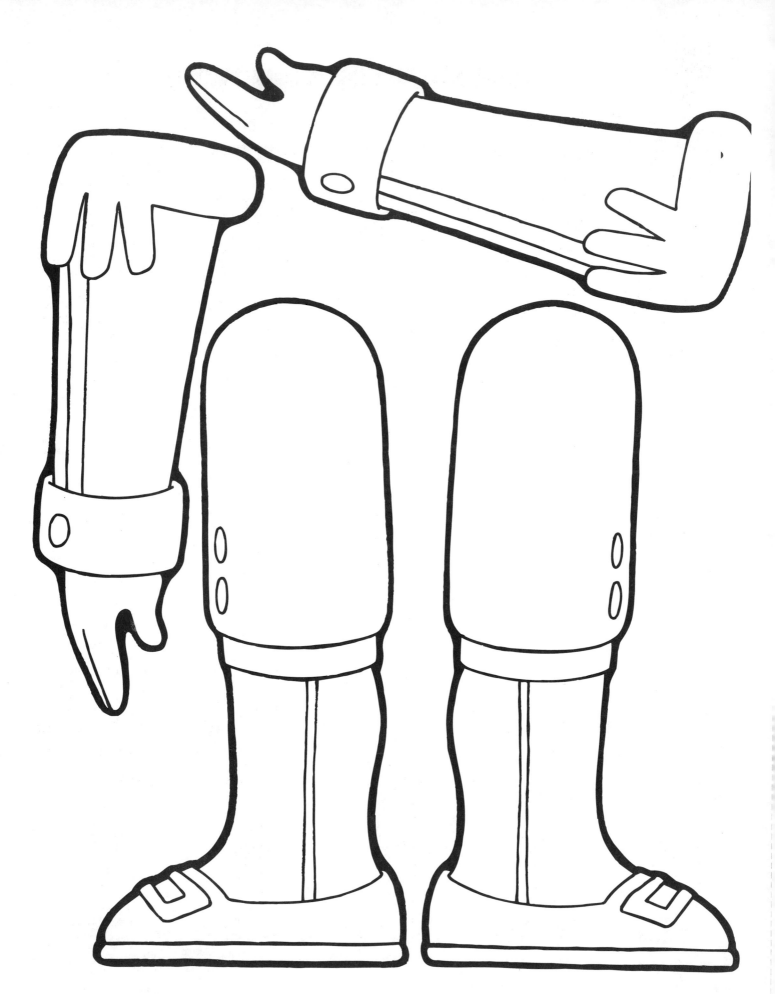

20

Learning with Nursery Rhymes • EMC 741

Soldiers for Counting

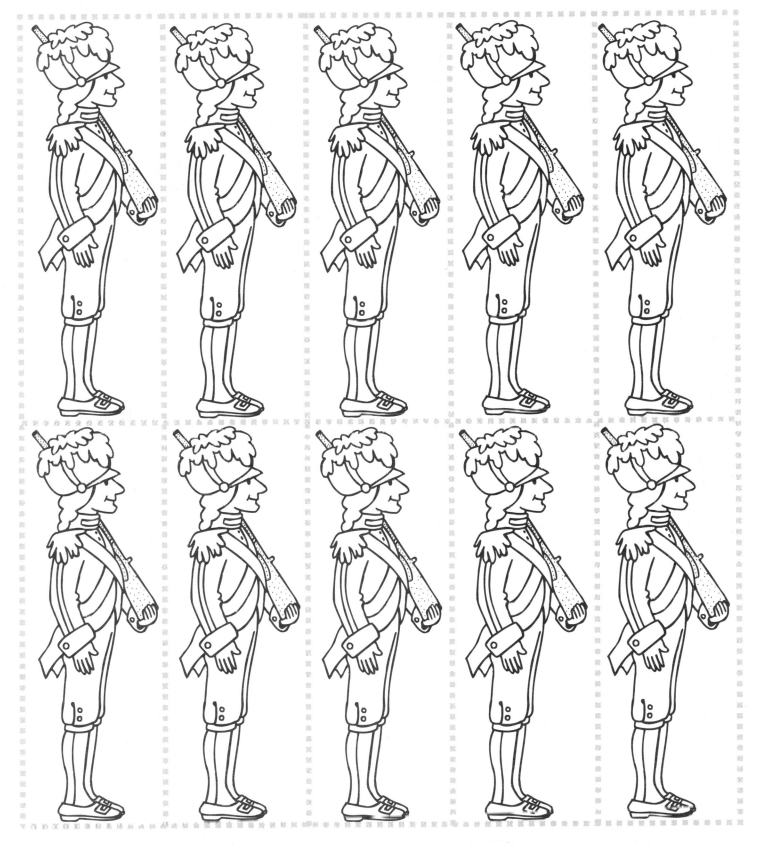

The Noble Duke of York

Oh, the noble Duke of York,

He had ten thousand men.

He marched them up to the top of the hill,

And he marched them down again.

Learning with Nursery Rhymes • EMC 741

Patty-Cake, Patty-Cake

Patty-cake, patty-cake, baker's man,

Bake me a cake as fast as you can.

Roll it and prick it and mark it with a B,

Put it in the oven for baby and me.

Children in England still eat pat-a-cakes. They are small cakes with currants. The original version may have used the word, Beker's-man, which was an old Saxon word for priest. Originally the words said "Mark it with T" which may have referred to making the sign of the cross over the wafer given at communion. The rhyme was printed as a children's song in Thomas d'Urfey's *The Campaigners* in 1698.

Using Patty-Cake in Your Classroom

LANGUAGE ARTS

Hearing the rhythm:

After reciting the rhyme, have students clap it so that they make one clap on each syllable. This may be difficult because they may be used to clapping one time for two or three syllables.

Demonstrate with patty-cake — pat ty cake = three claps. Slow the pace at first.
After students can clap the syllables have them walk the rhyme. (one step = one syllable)

Challenge students to listen for syllables by clapping words.
        cupcake   bakery   ingredients   mix   bake   oven

Try clapping and walking some of the new rhymes on page 27. You may even choose to make up your own phrases or rhymes.

Hearing the rhyme:

Make sure that your students understand what the term rhyme means. Words rhyme if the last part of the words is the same.
        H<u>ill</u>   B<u>ill</u>

Recite the rhyme and have students identify the rhyming words.
        cake and bake   man and can   B and me

Reproduce the practice page with rhyming pairs on page 28 if your students are ready for independent practice.

Sequencing:

An important part of retelling a rhyme is putting the events in the right sequence.
1. Reproduce the pictures on page 29.
2. Have students put the pictures in order to help the baker make the patty-cakes.
3. Number the steps.
4. For independent practice, have the students paste the pictures on a blank page and number them.
        1—Roll it   2—Prick it   3—Mark it   4—Put it in the oven

MATH

Measuring:

Talk about the importance of measuring to a baker.
Prepare a measuring center. You will need:

- four different containers — a drinking glass, a jar, a bowl, and a bottle
- some rice
- a small scoop
- record sheet (page 30)
- flat box or tray

A student chooses a container, sets it on the tray, and scoops the rice to fill it.
Then records the number of scoops on the record sheet.
When the student has filled each container, compare the information to determine which container holds the most and which holds the least.

Make your own patty-cakes:

Following this recipe, prepare the dough in front of the students. Allow them to assist measuring and stirring.

Mix together:

1 package of brown sugar
1 pound of butter
1 1/2 teaspoons of vanilla
4 1/2 cups of flour

Chill for at least 30 minutes.
Form cakes.
Bake at 300° for 15 minutes.

After the dough is prepared and chilled, students will "pat" their own cakes. They will move through three stations as described on page 26, finishing with a cake to put on a community tray for baking.

What you will need:

- mixing spoon
- cookie sheets
- full can of soda pop to use as a rolling pin
- waxed paper or baking parchment
- toothpicks

Getting Ready

Reproduce page 31.

Paste each section to an index card folded in half.

Place the standing cards along a table or counter to identify the three stations of the assembly line.

Cut a small square of waxed paper for each student.

Before beginning, students write name or initials on waxed paper squares. They will scoot this square along the table with their cake on top of it until they put the square and the cake on the baking sheet. Move a small number of students at a time through the assembly line. The rest of the students might be working on the activities on pages 28 and/or 29 while they wait their turns.

Station 1 Roll it!

Students will take a spoon full of dough out of mixing bowl.

Roll it in their hands to form a ball.

Place the ball of dough on waxed paper square.

Flatten the dough with the soda-can rolling pin.

Station 2 Mark it!

Students mark the cake with a toothpick.

They might write a B or use their own initials.

Station 3 Bake it!

Students place their waxed paper square with their cake on the cookie sheet to be baked.

SCIENCE

Changes:

Cooking is a great time to observe changes.

Look carefully at the ingredients that you use before cooking.

Draw pictures on the record sheet (page 32) to show the ingredients.

Then look carefully again after each step.

Have students describe these changes in their own words.

New Rhymes for Clapping

Lollipop, lollipop,

Sugar sweet

I want a treat

That's good to eat.

Hamburger, hamburger, on the grill

I'll eat my fill and pay the bill.

Spaghetti, spaghetti,

On my plate

Twisty or straight.

It tastes just great.

Broccoli, broccoli,

Who agrees

Baby trees taste

Better than plain

Green peas?

 Learning with Nursery Rhymes • EMC 741

Find the Rhyme

Cut and paste to show the rhyming pairs.

Help the Baker

Color, cut, and paste the steps in order.

1.	paste
2.	paste
3.	paste
4.	paste

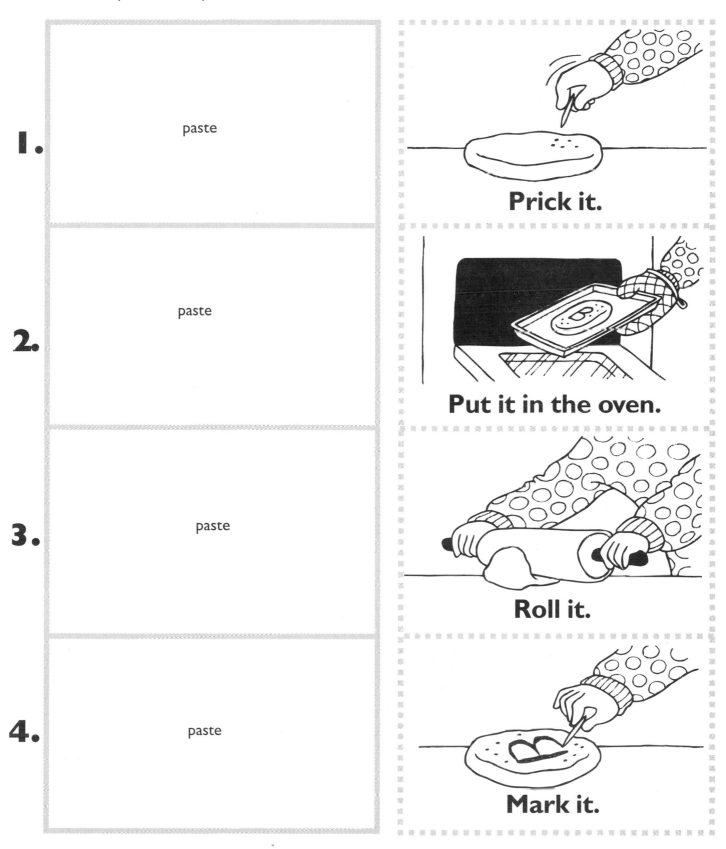

Prick it.

Put it in the oven.

Roll it.

Mark it.

How Many Scoops?

Record the number of scoops it takes to fill each container.

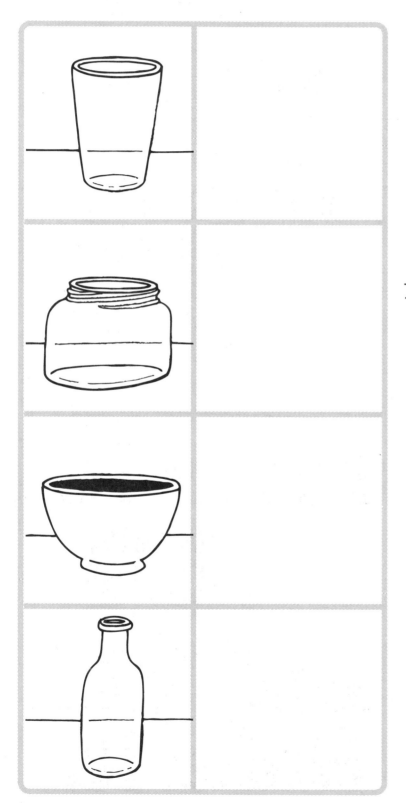

Which container holds the least?

Which container holds the most?

Learning with Nursery Rhymes • EMC 741

Let's Make Patty-Cakes

1. Cut out signs to place at each work station.

2. Glue to index cards.

3. Fold in half.

Roll it.

Mark it.

Bake it.

Changes I Noticed

Before	After
Before I rolled the dough out flat.	**After I rolled the dough out flat.**
Before I baked the cakes in the oven.	**After I baked the cakes in the oven.**

This Little Piggie

This little piggie went to market.

This little piggie stayed home.

This little piggie had roast beef.

This little piggie had none.

And this little piggie cried, "Wee! Wee! Wee!"

All the way home.

The piggie verse is a well-known toe-counting rhyme. It has many variants and is known in many different countries.

This little cow eats grass,

This little cow eats hay,

This little cow drinks water,

This little cow runs away,

And this little cow does nothing

But lie down all the day.

Chinese version

Using This Little Piggie in Your Classroom

LANGUAGE ARTS

Retell the story with puppets:
Reproduce the piggie finger puppets and the cow finger puppets on pages 36-37.
Use the puppets to retell the story.
Put the puppets in a center and encourage dramatic play.

Substitute new animals:
Reproduce the animal pictures on page 38.
Reread both versions of the rhyme, pointing out that different animals can be used.
Let students choose one of the pictured animals to star in the verse. Together, create
your own version of the verse. Don't worry about actually rhyming, but make the
animal's actions appropriate to its normal behavior.

This little monkey climbed a palm tree.
This little monkey stayed below.
This little monkey ate bananas.
This little monkey had none.
This little monkey cried "Chee! Chee! Chee!"
all through the jungle.

Substitute other animals to make
more new rhymes.

Sequence the story:
Reproduce, mount, and laminate the
picture cards on pages 39-41.
Use the cards to practice sequencing the story.

Real or make-believe:
Talk about whether the actions of the piggies could have been real
or whether they were make-believe.

Reproduce page 42 and have students identify
animal actions that are real.

Practice responding:

Reproduce page 43 to create a Where Did You Go? class book.
Have students draw their responses.

Then develop vocabulary by having students complete the phrase
"This little person went to _____."
Add the word that names their response.

Bind the pages together.
Have each student stand as you read their page aloud.

MATH

Counting:

Use the eight pigs on page 44 to practice counting.
Draw a pen and a puddle on a large sheet of paper.
Put some of the pigs in the pen and some in the puddle.
Ask students to tell how many pigs are in each place.
Then ask how many pigs there are in all.

Encourage students to create their own problems.

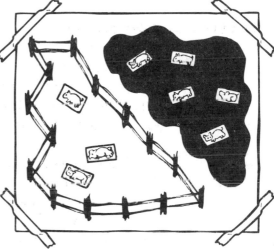

Sorting and grouping by attributes:

The pigs on page 44 can be divided by these attributes:

      happy/sad   moving/still   curly tail/straight tail   one eye showing/two eyes showing

Talk about the pictures with your students.
Have them identify the attributes.
Sort pigs into two groups according to the attributes.

      Put the happy pigs here.   Put the sad pigs here.

If your class is used to sorting by attributes, use Venn Diagrams.

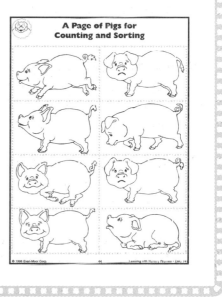

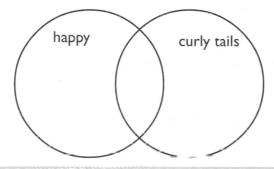

Piggie Finger Puppets

Make these puppets to use in retelling the rhyme.

1. Color

2. Cut

3. Fold in half.

4. Paste side closed.

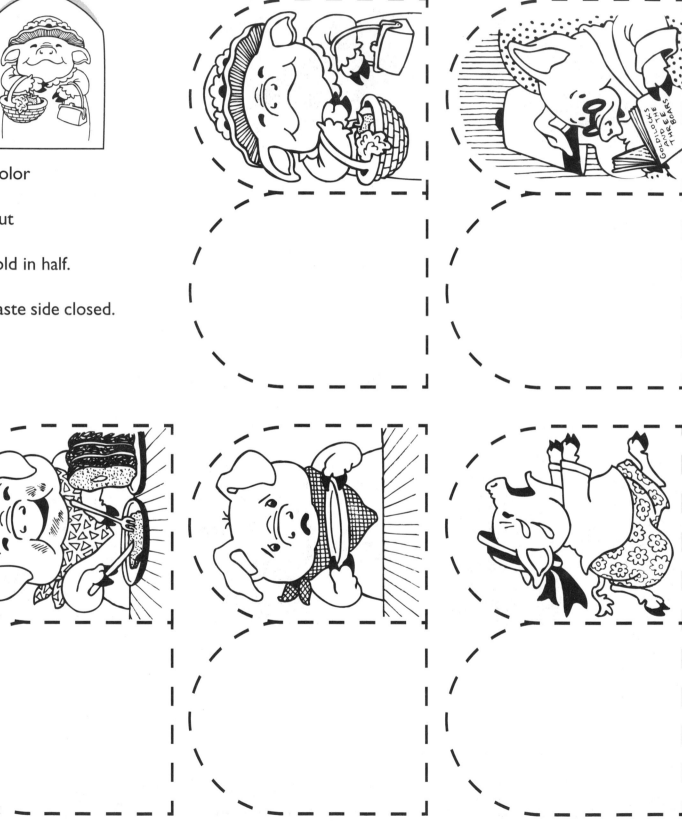

     Learning with Nursery Rhymes • EMC 741

Cow Finger Puppets

Make these puppets to retell the Chinese rhyme.

1. Color

2. Cut

3. Fold in half.

4. Paste side closed.

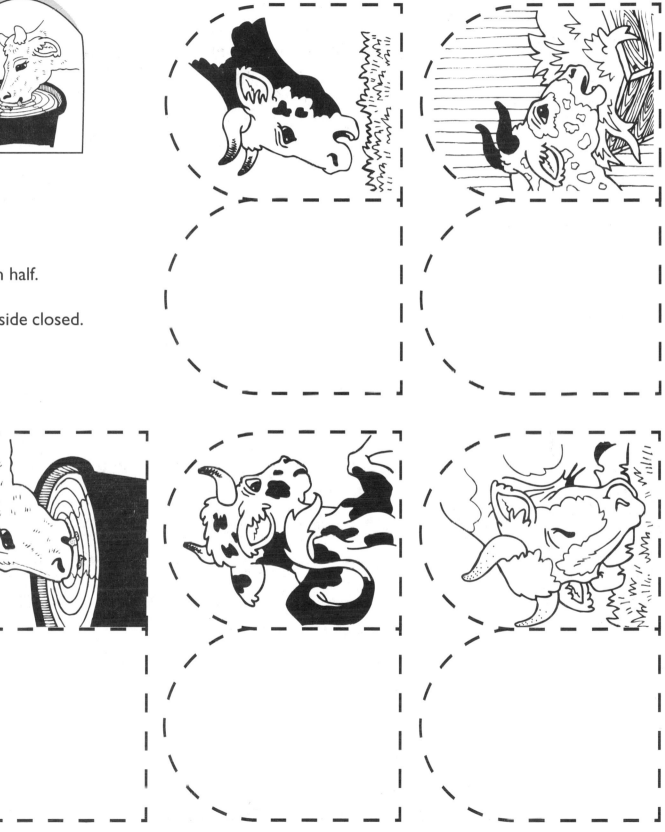

Making a New Rhyme

Use these picture cards to model how you might substitute new animals to make new rhymes. Encourage your students to substitute their own animals in new counting rhymes.

Picture Cards for Sequencing

Reproduce these cards for practice in sequencing.

The End

 Learning with Nursery Rhymes • EMC 741

Learning with Nursery Rhymes • EMC 741

Could It Be Real?

yes   no

yes   no

yes   no

yes   no

This little person went to

_____

Pigs for Counting and Sorting

Ride a Cock-Horse

Ride a cock-horse to Banbury Cross,

To see a fine lady upon a white horse.

Rings on her fingers and bells on her toes,

She shall have music whereever she goes.

This rhyme can be traced back to the 1600s. It might have referred to Queen Elizabeth I, Lady Godiva, or Celia Fiennes, a British horsewoman. Today the term *cock-horse* refers to a stick horse toy, but during the 16th century, a cock-horse was a large horse.

Using Ride a Cock-Horse in Your Classroom

LANGUAGE ARTS

Retelling the story — story board:

Reproduce the story board and stand ups on pages 48 and 49.
Use the board and horse stand-ups to retell the story.

Creative drama:

Make several stick ponies using the directions on page 50.
Set up a pony riding center.
Encourage students to ride their ponies to different
locations around the classroom and to tell what they saw.

Large and small:

Explain that cock-horse was a term for a large horse.
Use real things in your classroom and classify them as large or small.
Reproduce the picture cards on pages 51 and 52.
Sort the pictures into pairs and tell which of the two is
large and which is small.

MATH

Counting:

Reproduce the rings and bells on pages 53 and 54.
Use them for counting and simple computation.

One-to-one correspondence:

Practice one-to-one correspondence by matching
one ring to each finger and one bell to each toe.

Sorting:

Use the rings on page 53 for sorting.
(Attributes include plain bands, pearls, round stones, square stones, and rectangular stones.)

Smallest to biggest:

Reproduce the bells on page 54 for ordering.

Talk about size differences.

Have five students arrange themselves from shortest to tallest.

Repeat with five other students.

Then demonstrate using the bell pictures.

When students are ready, have them arrange the bells from smallest to biggest as an independent activity.

BEGINNING MAP SKILLS

Make a masking tape crossroads on the floor.

Designate locations—a castle, farm, home, woods—at the end points of each road.

Have students ride stick horses along the roads as you give directions.

"Trot down the road to the castle."

"Go to the crossroads and then turn to go to the woods."

Draw a simple map of your crossroads set-up.
Use the stand-up horses and rider from page 48.
Move the horse on the map just as the students moved on the floor.

Introduce the terms right and left when appropriate for your class.

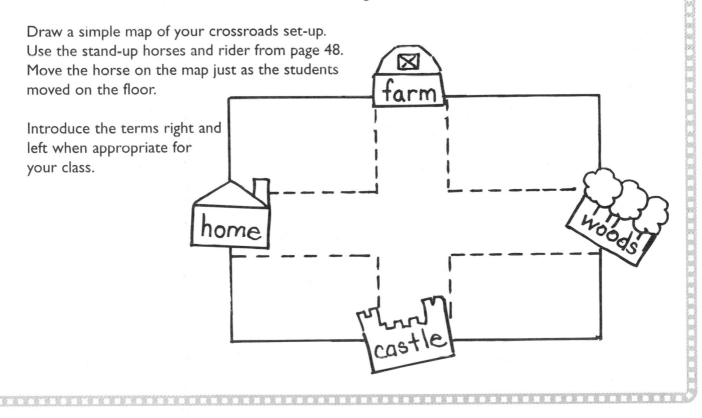

Ride a Cock-Horse Storyboard

fold

Cock-Horse

a

Ride

fold

fold

fold

Cock-Horse

a

Ride

fold

fold

Ride a Cock-Horse

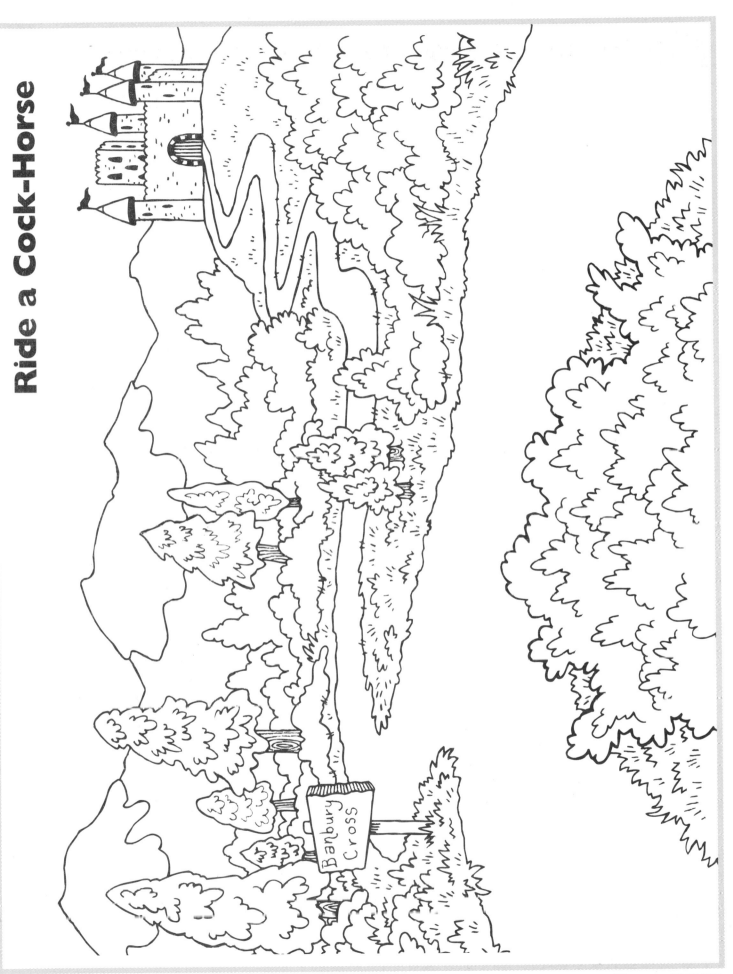

Banbury Cross

Learning with Nursery Rhymes • EMC 741

Stick Horse

Materials:

- old sock
- stuffing—plastic grocery sacks work well
- felt for features
- yarn for mane
- sewing needle
- 3-foot piece of large-diameter doweling or old broom stick
- wide package tape
- thin rope for reins
- glue—a hot-glue gun is best, but is not to be used by children

Directions:

1. Stuff the sock with stuffing.

2. Insert stick into sock. It should extend to the heel.

3. Tape the sock to the stick around the lower edge.

4. Cut eyes and ears from felt and glue to sock.

5. Sew yarn to back side of sock for mane.

6. Add rope for reins. Tie the rope around the horse's nose and loop back over stick. Tie the two ends together.

7. Ride off into the sunset...

Learning with Nursery Rhymes • EMC 741

Ride a Cock-Horse Picture Cards

Learning with Nursery Rhymes • EMC 741

Rings for Counting and Sorting

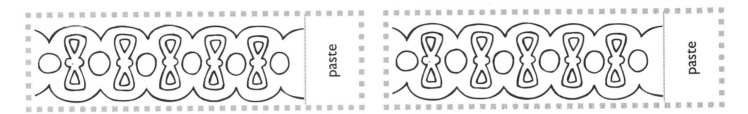

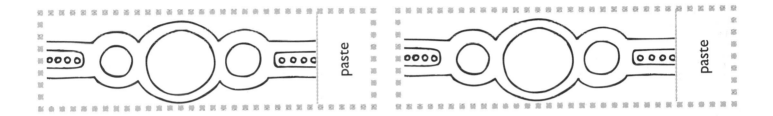

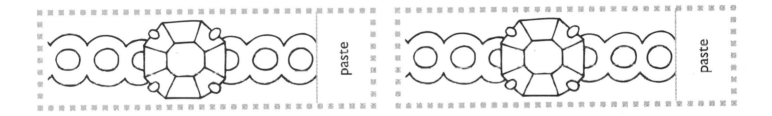

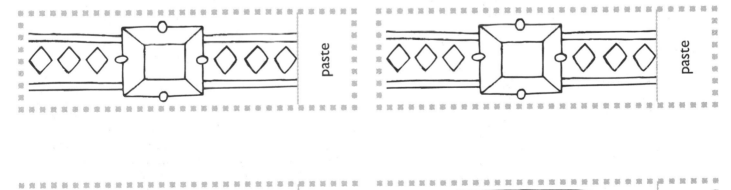

Learning with Nursery Rhymes • EMC 741

Bells for Counting and Sorting

Learning with Nursery Rhymes • EMC 741

Hickory Dickory Dock

Hickory dickory dock,

The mouse ran up the clock.

The clock struck one, and down he run.

Hickory dickory dock.

This rhyme was first published as a limerick in *Tom Thumb's Pretty Song Book*, 1744.

Using Hickory Dickory Dock
in Your Classroom

LANGUAGE ARTS

Retelling:

Reproduce and prepare the mouse headband on page 58.
Choose a child to play the part of the mouse in the retelling
of the rhyme. Designate a clock (perhaps a chair or a table).
Have the class chant, "Hickory dickory dock" in a steady
rhythm to imitate the ticking of the clock as you recite the
verse and the mouse acts it out.

Up and down:

Reproduce the clock pattern on page 59 and the flaps for the clock
on page 57.

After students have put their clocks together, use them to review the
sight words, up and down. (Word cards are on page 11.)
Show a word card and have the students open the door representing
up or down. Confirm the right choice by comparing the word on the clock with
the word card.

Where did he run?

Discuss all the places that a mouse might run.
Reproduce the book page on page 60 for individual students.
Have students draw to show where they think the mouse ran.
Add words to the pages.
Bind the pages together to make a class book.
Read the book together and enjoy the creativity of your students.
Put the book in your classroom library for daily browsing.

A new verse:

Reproduce the Hickory Dickory Book on pages 61- 63.
Make the pages into a little book or make transparencies of each page.
Add a construction paper cover. Read the regular verse (page 1 of the book).
Have students identify the rhyme pattern in the regular verse (one—run).

Explain that you have several new verses that tell what the mouse did when the clock struck
different hours.

Read each new verse and have students identify the new rhymes.

(two-shoe, three-knee, four-floor, five-dive, six-tricks)

Make up new verses following the same rhyme pattern.

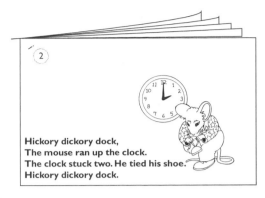

Hickory dickory dock,
The mouse ran up the clock.
The clock stuck two. He tied his shoe.
Hickory dickory dock.

MATH

Counting strikes:

Pretend that you are a bonging clock. Tap a vase or make the bong noise yourself.
Ask students to count the numbers of bongs and tell what time it is.

Bong. Bong. Bong.   The clock struck three!

Telling time:

Bring in several different types of clocks and watches.
Have students identify the similarities and differences between the time pieces.
If your students are ready, now would be a good time to use your model clocks to practice reading the time. Since many homes may have only digital clocks, it is very important to read the hour on an analog clock as well.

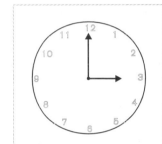

What do you do?

Help students relate time to their own lives.
Talk about what happens at different hours during your school day.
At 9 o'clock the bell rings, and we come inside to start our day.

Have students tell about different times that are significant to them outside of the school day.
Every night at 8 o'clock I go to bed.
My dad's alarm rings at 6 o'clock every morning.

Record student responses on a chart.

Flaps for Clock

Cut out these flaps and paste the top fold to the boxes of the clock on page 59.

peek

peek

Mouse Headband

1. Cut out the headband.
2. Cut two additional strips 2" x 4" (5 x 10 cm) from construction paper. Paste to ends of headband.
3. Insert a paper fastener near each end. Loop the ends of a rubber band around the head of each fastener to allow for variations in fit.

1. Color
2. Cut out the flaps
3. Paste the flaps

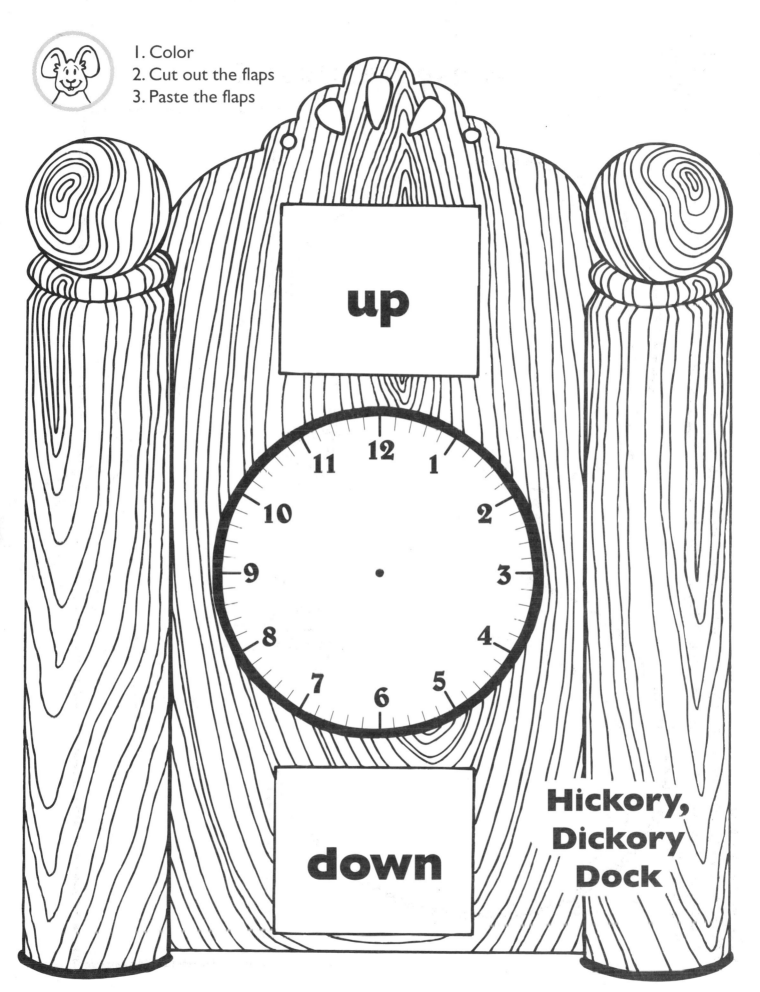

up

12 11 1 10 2 9 3 8 4 7 6 5

down

Hickory,
Dickory
Dock

Learning with Nursery Rhymes • EMC 741

Where Did the Mouse Go?

The mouse ran _____

_____

Hickory Dickory

Hickory dickory dock,

The mouse ran up the clock.

The clock struck one, and down he run.

Hickory dickory dock.

   Learning with Nursery Rhymes • EMC 741

---

②

Hickory dickory dock,

The mouse ran up the clock.

The clock struck two. He tied his shoe.

Hickory dickory dock.

   Learning with Nursery Rhymes • EMC 741

3

Hickory dickory dock,

The mouse ran up the clock.

The clock struck three. He bumped his knee.

Hickory dickory dock.

4

Hickory dickory dock,

The mouse ran up the clock.

The clock struck four. He jumped to the floor.

Hickory dickory dock.

Hickory dickory dock,

The mouse ran up the clock.

The clock struck five. He took a dive.

Hickory dickory dock.

6

Hickory dickory dock,

The mouse ran up the clock.

The clock struck six. He did some tricks.

Hickory dickory dock.

Brow Bender, Eye Peeper

Brow Bender,

Eye Peeper,

Nose Dropper,

Mouth Eater,

Chin Chopper,

Knock at the door,

Ring the bell,

Lift up the latch,

Walk in,

Take a chair,

Sit by there,

And how do you do this morning?

This English rhyme counts features in a fanciful way usually accompanied by giggles from the one being "counted on." The first four lines were published in *Tommy Thumb's Song Book*, 1788.

Using Brow Bender, Eye Peeper in Your Classroom

LANGUAGE ARTS

Label the child:

As you introduce this rhyme, point to the features named.

brow bender = forehead
eye peeper = eye
nose dropper = nose
mouth eater = mouth
chin chopper = chin

Enlarge the figure on page 67 or use it as a transparency and have students point with the pointer (page 68) as the rhyme is repeated.

Definitions:

After enjoying this rhyme initiate a conversation about definitions.

"What is a definition?" "Does this rhyme have anything to do with definitions?"
Help students to see that "eye peeper" is really a kind of definition—eyes peep, or look.

Try making up some new words that describe other body parts.

foot kicker   elbow poker   tongue licker

Add these new parts to your rhyme and practice pointing them out.

Following directions

Make reciting the rhyme a game.
Designate the layout of an imagined house.
"Here's the door. This is the kitchen. Here is the chair by the table."
Choose a student to act out the rhyme as it is repeated.
Start slowly.
The student points to the feature named for the first part of the rhyme.
Then the student pretends to

knock on the door,
ring the doorbell,
lift the latch.

The student walks through the pretend doorway, takes a chair, and says
"How do you do this morning?" with the group.
After you have practiced the routine slowly, try speeding it up!

Adding -er to words:

Help students recognize the significance of the suffix -er.
Ask students to name some of the things that they can do.

"I can run."   "I can write."   "I can draw."

Write a label for each child using the word + er.

runner   writer   drawer

Ask students to tell you what is the same about each word.
(Each word has -er at the end.)
Check for understanding by asking questons such as:

"What would you call a person who can read?" (reader)
"What would you call a person who can sing?" (singer)

Creating a picture dictionary:

Apply this new knowledge about definitions and adding -er by creating
a picture dictionary.

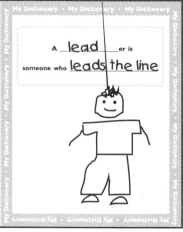

Reproduce the blank dictionary page (page 69) for every student.
Have students draw themselves doing something in your classroom.
Then help the students to complete the definition part of the page.

A leader is someone who leads the line.
A helper is someone who helps clean up.
A writer is someone who writes a story.

67 Learning with Nursery Rhymes • EMC 741

Pointer Pattern

To make this pointer last:
- Reproduce the pattern.
- Color and cut it out.
- Laminate the cutout.
- Fold the pattern in half.
- Attach a dowel to the inside of one side of the pattern.
- Fold the other side over.
- Tape to hold the pointer pattern closed.

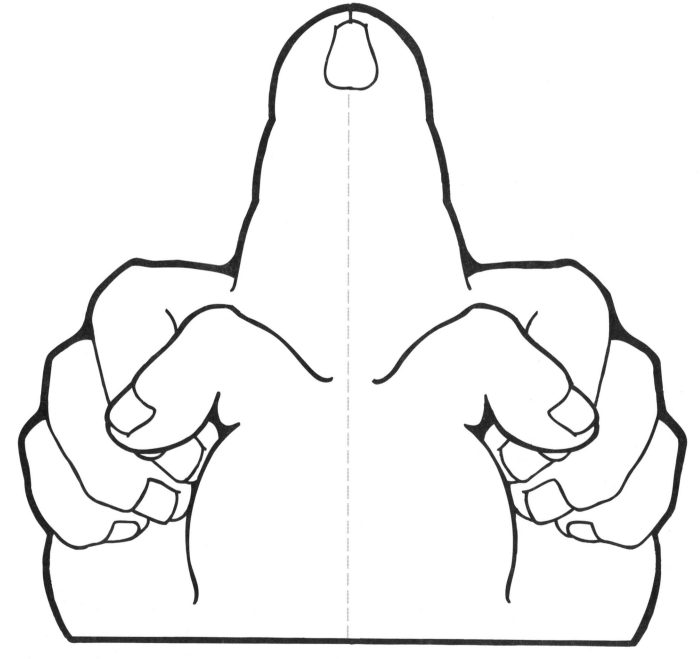

A _____er is

someone who _____.

Twinkle, Twinkle

Twinkle, twinkle little star,

How I wonder what you are.

Up above the world so high.

Like a diamond in the sky.

Twinkle, twinkle little star,

How I wonder what you are.

While we usually recite or sing the verse as its printed here, the original rhyme was much longer and included the following verses:

When the blazing sun is gone,
When he nothing shines upon,
Then you show your little light,
Twinkle, twinkle, all the night.

When the traveler in the dark,
Thanks you for your tiny spark,
He could not see which way to go,
If you did not twinkle so.

In the dark blue sky you keep,
And often through my curtains peep,
For you never shut your eye,
'Till the sun is in the sky.

As your bright and tiny spark,
Lights the traveler in the dark, - - -
Though I know not what you are,
Twinkle, twinkle, little star.

Using Twinkle, Twinkle in Your Classroom

LANGUAGE ARTS

Special comparisons:

After you have recited and sung *Twinkle, Twinkle*, have students notice the comparison that is made in the rhyme.

> A star is like a diamond in the sky.

This comparison is a simile, an important tool of figurative language. While your students do not need to know the term simile, they can certainly begin making these special comparisons.

Have them compare two unlike things by using the words "is like."
> The grass is like a green carpet.
> Spaghetti is like slippery worms.

Reproduce the activity sheet on page 73 and have students draw to complete each comparison. Add the words as they tell you about their work.

I wonder...:

The long-ago author of *Twinkle Twinkle* wondered about what a star really was.
Take the time to talk with your students about some of the things that they wonder about.
Make a chart to post in the room and add "I wonders" as they are mentioned.

/st/ Words:

Gather several objects or pictures that begin with the st- blend (stapler, stick, stool, stop sign, stone) and several that do not.

Show the objects to your students and ask them to identify the ones that begin with the same sound as star. Have students say the name of the object aloud and then repeat star.

For independent practice in identifying things that begin with the same sound as star, reproduce the activity sheet on page 74.

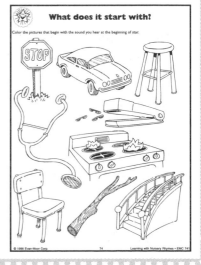

Just for fun:

Reproduce the pattern on page 75 for individual students. Have them color, cut, and paste to make their own star spinners.

It's fun to twirl the spinner back and forth in your hands making the star "twinkle" as you recite the rhyme.

A puzzling night:

Reproduce the puzzle on page 76 to use in a classroom center or as a take-home game for individual students.

Color the picture, cut the pieces apart, and then put it together again.

To make the pieces last longer, mount them on poster board after coloring. Laminate the puzzle before cutting the pieces apart.

MATH

Stars in the sky:

Use the star counters on page 77 for counting and simple computation.

After using the stars as counters, you may want to make a counting book:
1. Cut 8 1/2" x 11" (21.5 x 28 cm) paper into fourths.
2. Give each student six of these quarter sheets.
3. The first sheet will be the title page.
4. Label the remaining pages 0, 1, 2, 3, and 4.
5. Glue stars on the pages to show each number.
6. Staple the pages together to make a book.

SCIENCE

What is a star?

Now would be a great time to read some of the wonderful fiction and nonfiction literature about stars.

Astronomy by Kristen Lippincott; Dorling Kindersley, 1994.
Little Rabbit Goes to Sleep by Tony Johnston; HarperCollins, 1994.
My Place in Space by Robin and Sally Hirst; Orchard Books, 1990.
Night Goes By by Kate Spohn; Macmillan Books for Young Readers, 1995.
Night Sky by Carole Stott; Dorling Kindersley, 1993.
The Night Sky by Robin Kerrod; Benchmark Books, 1996.
Sing to the Stars by Mary Brigid; Little, Brown, 1994.
Starry Night by David Spohn; Lothrop, Lee and Shepard, 1992.
The Sun and the Stars by Lesley Sims; Raintree Steck-Vaughn, 1995.
Twinkle, Twinkle Little Star by Jane Taylor; Morrow Junior Books, 1992.

Making Comparisons

is like

is like

What Does It Start With?

Color the pictures that begin with the sound you hear at the beginning of ⭐ star .

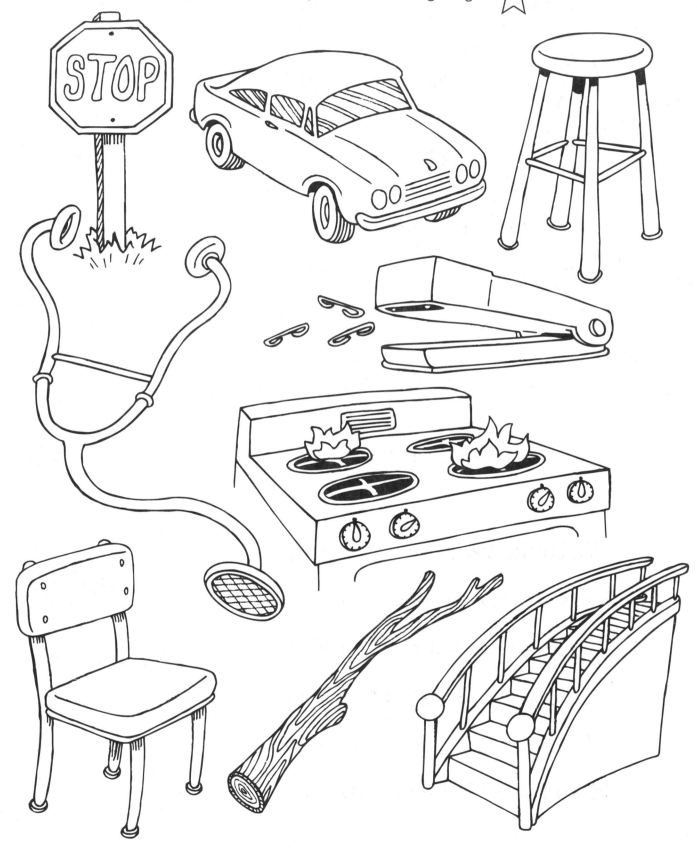

Learning with Nursery Rhymes • EMC 741

A Spinning Star

Twinkle, Twinkle

Twinkle, twinkle little star,

How I wonder what you are.

Up above the world so high.

Like a diamond in the sky.

Twinkle, twinkle little star,

How I wonder what you are.

1. Color

2. Cut

3. Fold

4. Tape

5. Paste shut

Learning with Nursery Rhymes • EMC 741

Starry Night Puzzle

Learning with Nursery Rhymes • EMC 741

Stars for Counting

Learning with Nursery Rhymes • EMC 741

Humpty Dumpty

Humpty Dumpty sat on a wall,

Humpty Dumpty had a great fall,

All the King's horses, and all the King's men,

Couldn't put Humpty Dumpty together again.

This riddle-rhyme about an egg first appeared in *Gammer Gurton's Garland* in 1810. The original version read:

> Humpty Dumpty sat on a wall,
> Humpty Dumpty had a great fall;
> Three score men and three score more,
> Cannot place Humpty Dumpty as he was before.

Children in France call Humpty, "Boule, Boule." In Sweden he's known as "Thille Lille"; in Denmark, "Lille-Trill"; in Finland, "Hillerin-Lillerin"; and in Switzerland, "Annenadadeli."

Using Humpty Dumpty in Your Classroom

LANGUAGE ARTS

Sequencing:
Reproduce the three picture cards on page 80.
Have students sequence the cards to retell the story.

Rhyming:
Have students identify the rhyming words in the verse.
    wall—fall   men—again

Reproduce the picture bricks on pages 81-83 and build
rhyming walls with the class:
For younger groups,
- Choose a brick.
- Name the picture. (boat)
- Find a rhyming picture on a second brick. (coat)
  Put the second brick on top of the first.
- Add additional rhyming bricks to build a rhyming wall.

MATH

Beginning word problems:
Reproduce the picture cards on pages 84 and 85.
Use the pictures to illustrate simple word problems.
    Three king's men stood guard.
    One marched away.
    How many are standing guard now?

SCIENCE
All the king's men couldn't put Humpty Dumpty together once he
was broken.

Ask students to name other things that change when they are broken
so that they can't be put back together again.

Reproduce the activity page on page 86 and have students tell whether
the things pictured could be put back together.

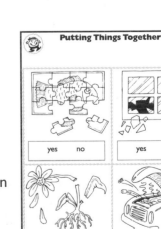

Picture Cards for Sequencing

Picture Bricks
for Building a Rhyming Wall

Learning with Nursery Rhymes • EMC 741

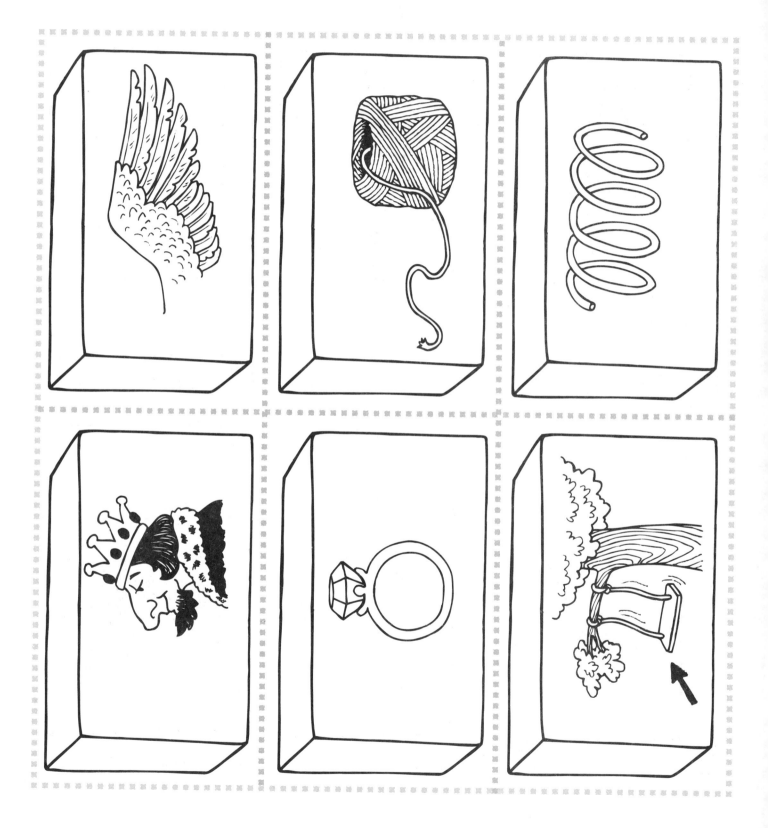

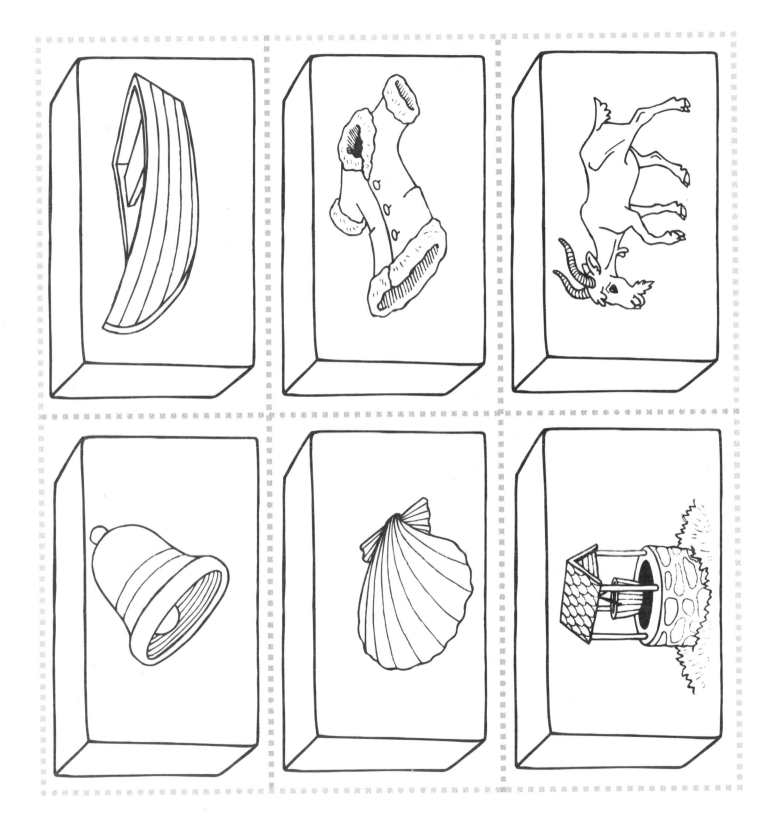

Figures for Counting

Learning with Nursery Rhymes • EMC 741

Putting Things Together

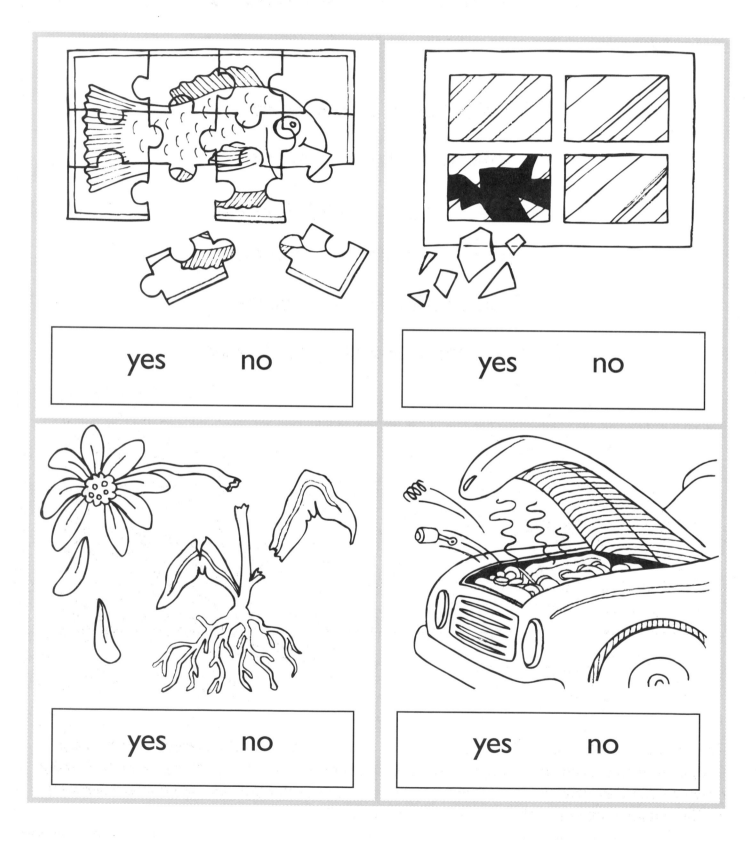

yes   no

yes   no

yes   no

yes   no

Old Mother Hubbard

Old Mother Hubbard

Went to the cupboard

To get her poor dog a bone;

But when she got there

The cupboard was bare,

And so the poor dog had none.

The rhyme Old Mother Hubbard probably originated with Sarah Catherine Martin. She is said to have chattered so incessantly that her brother in law told her to run away and write down one of her little rhymes instead of talking to him. The result was *The Comic Adventures of Old Mother Hubbard and Her Dog*, published in 1805.

Using Mother Hubbard in Your Classroom

LANGUAGE ARTS
Retelling the story:

Reproduce the dog headband on page 89.
Have students wear it while retelling of the story. Have other students play the part of Old Mother Hubbard. Provide aprons, shawls, head scarves, etc. as props.

Words that mean more than one thing:

Show your class a stuffed bear and asked them what it is.
Then repeat these lines of the rhyme:

And when she got there, the cupboard was bare.

bare   bear

Tell the students that bare and bear, although they sound the same, are spelled differently and mean different things.
Show the picture/word cards (page 90) for bare and bear and discuss the meanings.
Reproduce the activity sheet on page 91 and have students paste the correct word under each picture.

Vocabulary development — food for the cupboard:

Reproduce Mother Hubbard's cupboard and the food on pages 92-93.
Prepare the patterns for use on a flannel or magnetic board.
Begin to recite the verse and have a student select a food card to see what food Mother Hubbard is looking for.

Old Mother Hubbard went to the cupboard
To get her poor dog some <u>milk</u>.

Ask, "Do you think the dog would like milk?"
Place the food card in the correct column in the cupboard.
Continue until all foods have been placed in the cupboard.

Where else will she go?

Pages 94 and 95 provides a number of additional verses from the original rhyme. Share these examples with your students.
Have your students think of new places that Mother Hubbard might go and what she might get for her dog.
If your students are ready, reproduce the activity sheet on page 96 and have them draw to show where Mother Hubbard might go and what she might buy. Bind the pages into a class book.

What will Mother Hubbard get for her dog tomorrow?

She'll go to the_____

To get him a _____.

MATH

Bones for counting and computation are found on page 97.

Dog Headband

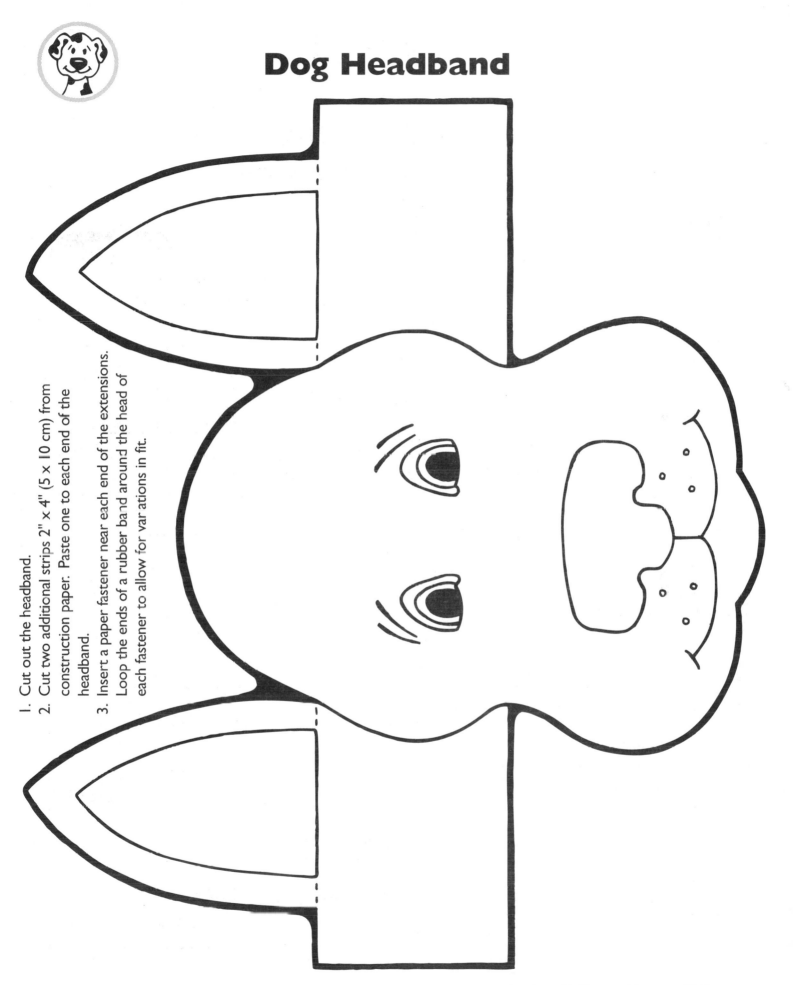

1. Cut out the headband.
2. Cut two additional strips 2" x 4" (5 x 10 cm) from construction paper. Paste one to each end of the headband.
3. Insert a paper fastener near each end of the extensions. Loop the ends of a rubber band around the head of each fastener to allow for variations in fit.

Learning with Nursery Rhymes • EMC 741

bear

bare

Bare or Bear

Cut ✂ Paste 🗒 paste

paste

paste

paste

paste

bare

bear

bare

bear

Old Mother Hubbard's Cupboard

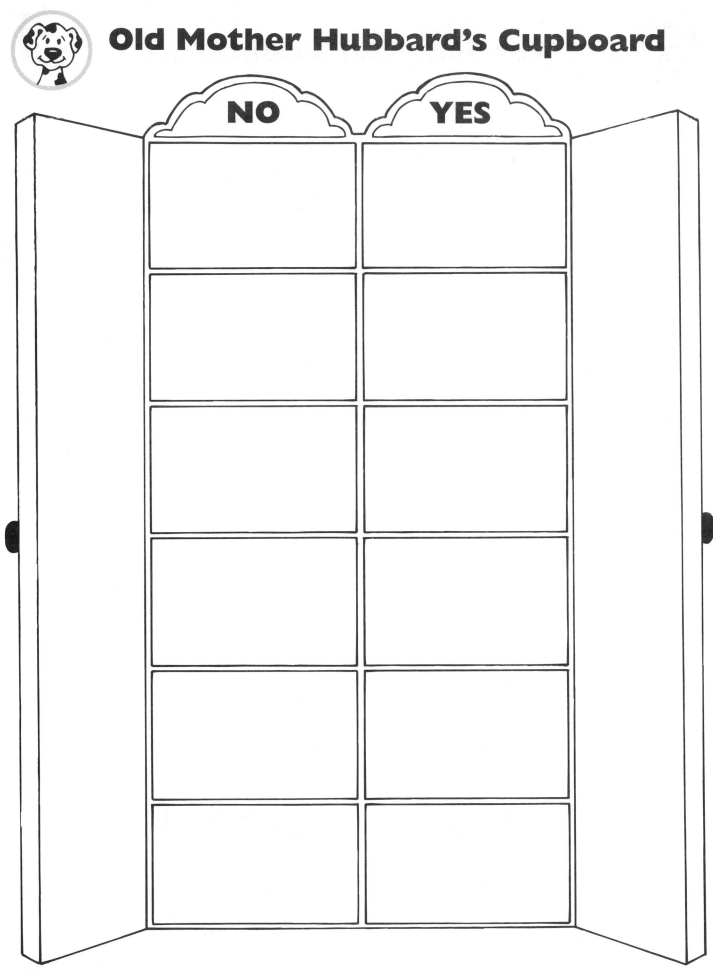

NO   YES

92

Food for the Cupboard

Old Mother Hubbard Verses

Some versions of this rhyme include many verses that tell about all
the places that Mother Hubbard went to get things for her dog.

Old Mother Hubbard
Went to the cupboard
To get her poor dog a bone;
But when she got there
The cupboard was bare,
And so the poor dog had none.

She went to the baker's
To buy him some bread;
But when she came back
The poor dog was dead.

She went to the undertaker's
To buy him a coffin;
But when she came back
The poor dog was laughing.

She took a clean dish
To get him some tripe;
But when she came back
He was smoking a pipe.

She went to the fishmonger's
To buy him some fish;
But when she came back
He was washing the dish.

She went to the hatter's
To buy him a hat;
But when she came back
He was feeding the cat.

She went to the barber's
To buy him a wig;
But when she came back
He was dancing a jig.

She went to the fruiterer's
To buy him some fruit;
But when she came back
He was playing the flute.

She went to the cobbler's
To buy him some shoes;
But when she came back
He was reading the news.

She went to the hosier's
To buy him some hose;
But when she came back
He was dressed in his clothes.

The dame made a curtsy,
The dog made a bow;
The dame said, "Your servant,"
The dog said, "Bow-wow."

What will Mother Hubbard get for her dog tomorrow?

She'll go to the_____

To get him a _____.

Bones for Counting

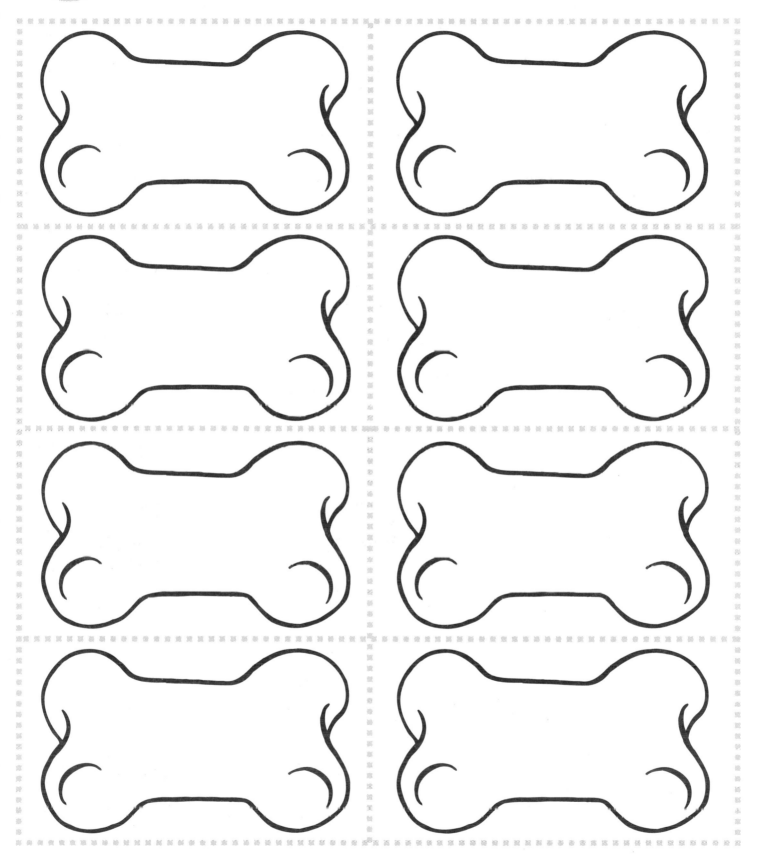

Learning with Nursery Rhymes • EMC 741

Little Boy Blue

Little Boy Blue
Come blow your horn,
The sheep's in the meadow,
The cow's in the corn.

Where is the boy
Who looks after the sheep?
He's under a haystack,
Fast asleep.

Will you wake him?
No, not I,
For if I do,
He's sure to cry.

Little Boy Blue might have been written about Thomas Cardinal Wolsey who was the Chief Minister of Henry VIII. He was a very demanding person and was disliked by the general public.

Using Little Boy Blue
in Your Classroom

LANGUAGE ARTS

Comprehension:

Reproduce pages 100 and 101 for each child. Cut and fold to create a standup haystack, sheep, and cow.

Check your students' comprehension by asking questions about the rhyme.

"Show me where the cow is."

"Where should the haystack go?"

"Where will you put the sheep?"

Retelling the story:

Use pages 100 and 101 again. Students manipulate the characters as they retell the story.

After they have a clear understanding of the rhyme, encourage them to make up a story of their own using the same characters.

MATH

A page of stand-up sheep (page 102) and a page of stand-up cows (page 103) have been provided for beginning counting and computation activities.

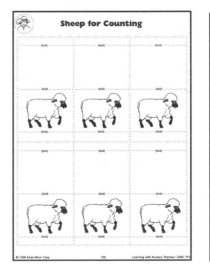

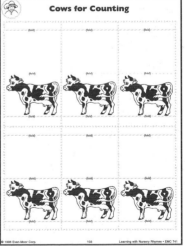

Little Boy Blue

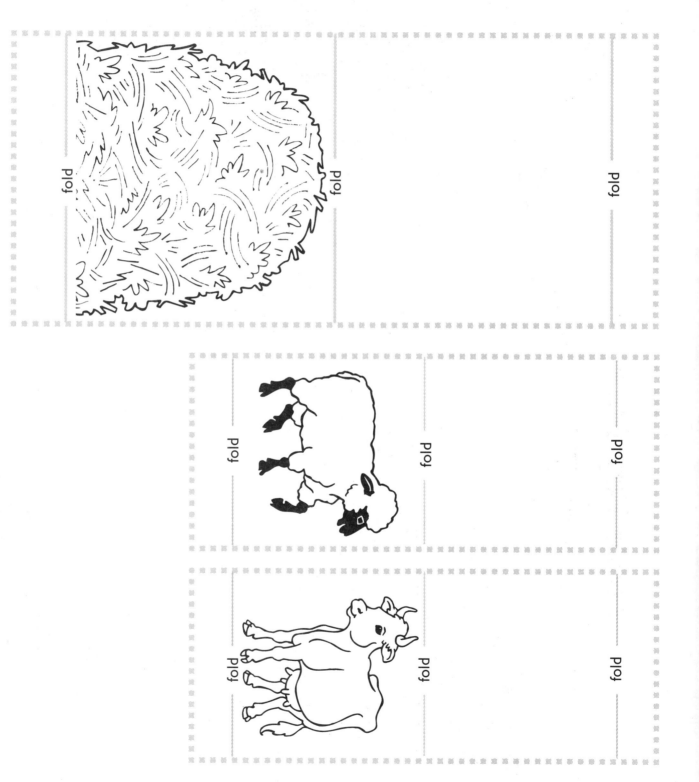

fold

fold

fold

fold

fold

fold

fold

fold

Learning with Nursery Rhymes • EMC 741

Little Boy Blue

Learning with Nursery Rhymes • EMC 741

Sheep for Counting

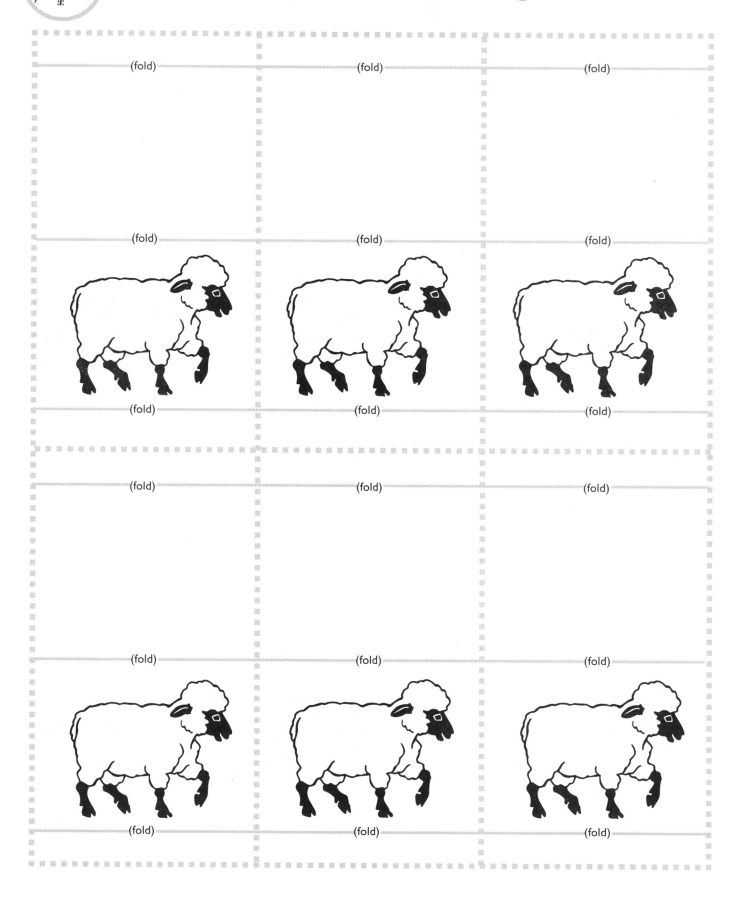

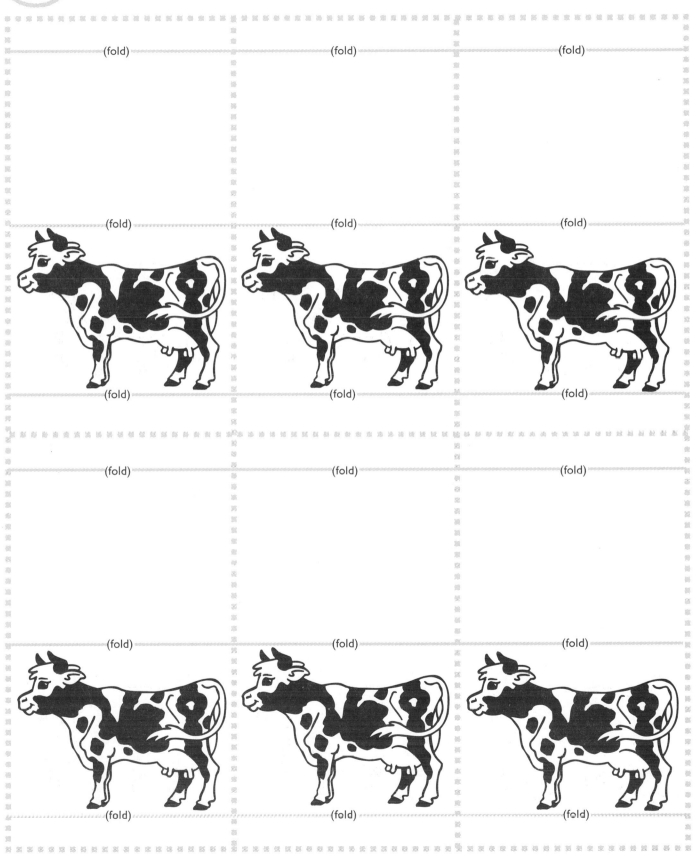

(fold)   (fold)   (fold)

(fold)   (fold)   (fold)

(fold)   (fold)   (fold)

(fold)   (fold)   (fold)

(fold)   (fold)   (fold)

(fold)   (fold)   (fold)

Hey Diddle Diddle

Hey, diddle, diddle!

The cat and the fiddle,

The cow jumped over the moon;

The little dog laughed

To see such sport,

And the dish ran away with the spoon.

At the time this rhyme was written, the late 1500s, public officials were often given animal nicknames. The cat in this rhyme is probably Elizabeth I who "played her cabinet as if they were mice." The dish was the name given to the servant who carried the golden dishes into the state dining room. The spoon was the beautiful young woman chosen by the court to be the "taster."

How to Use Hey Diddle Diddle in Your Classroom

LANGUAGE ARTS

Retelling and sequencing:
Reproduce the picture cards on page 106 to help in retelling and sequencing this rhyme.

Riddles:
Young students love riddles. Use their interest to help them to accurately describe an object and to give good clues so that someone else can guess what it is.

Tell the class that you are going to play a guessing game:
> "I will tell you three things about an object in our classroom. Then I'll ask you to guess what it is."

Demonstrate using the riddles below or make up your own.

It is red, white, and blue.	It is empty in the morning and
It has stars.	full at the end of the day.
It hangs on a stick.	It is metal.
What is it?	We put things we don't want in it.
	What is it?

As a class, write several riddles. If your students are ready, reproduce page 107 and help the students to draw and write their own riddles.

Just for fun:
Reproduce pages 108 and 109 on construction paper.
Follow the directions to make a Hey Diddle Diddle Wheel.

MATH

What's in the middle?:
Play a riddle game to identify the missing numbers.
Write a sequence of three numbers, but leave the middle number out. 1, _____, 3
Say "Hey Diddle Diddle! What's in the middle?"
Students respond with the correct number.
For independent practice, reproduce page 110 and have students complete the page.

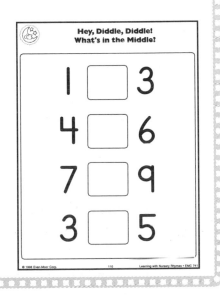

Hey Diddle Diddle Picture Cards

Learning with Nursery Rhymes • EMC 741

Hey Diddle Diddle
Can You Guess the Riddle?

Clue 1

Clue 2

Clue 3

What is it?

(fold up)

Answer

Hey, Diddle, Diddle Wheel

1. Color pages 108 and 109.

2. Cut out the half circle above the moon
   on page 109. Fold the page in half.
   Make the hole for the fastener.

3. Cut out the cow wheel on this page.
   Make the hole for the fastener.
   Place the wheel inside the folded page so that
   the cow shows through the hole and the holes line up.
   The wheel will protrude from the folder a bit.

4. Fasten the wheel with a paper fastener, pushing it
   through the back of the folder.

Insert fastener

here.

                                       Learning with Nursery Rhymes • EMC 741

Hey, diddle, diddle!
The cat and the fiddle.
The cow jumped over the moon;

Cut out this half circle.

The little dog laughed
To see such sport,
And the dish ran away with the spoon.

(fold)

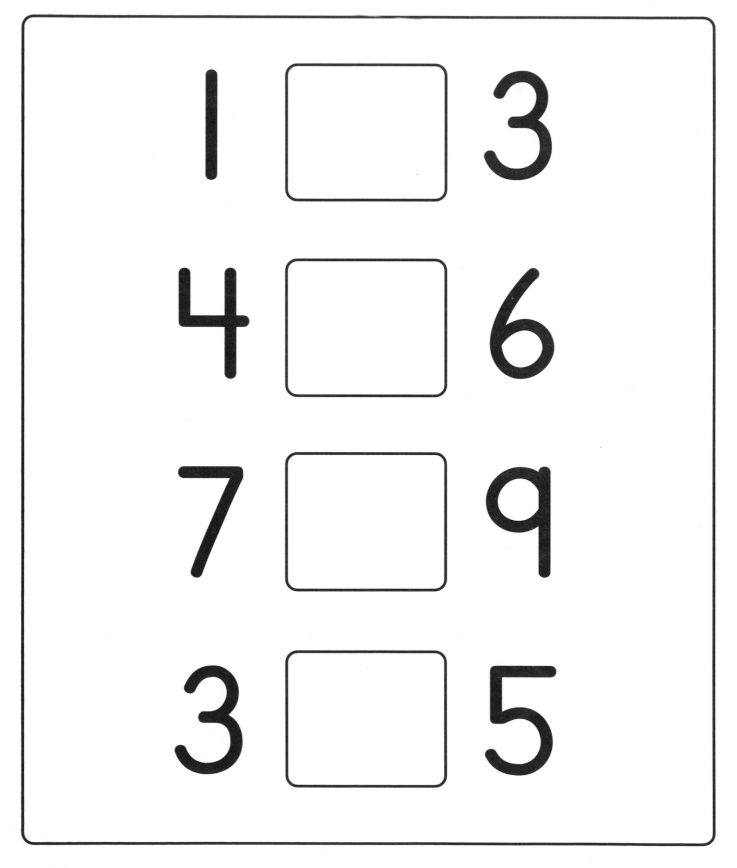

1 ☐ 3

4 ☐ 6

7 ☐ 9

3 ☐ 5

Note: Directions for using this page are on page 2.

 Know Your Rhymes ·······

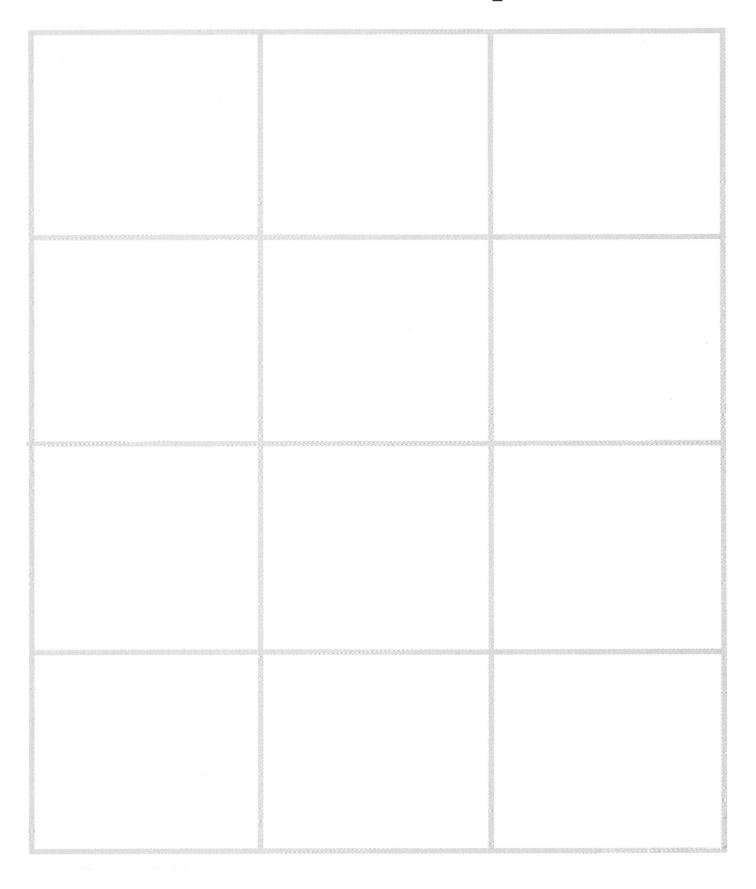

Note: Directions for using this page are on page 2.

Pictures for Knowing Your Rhymes